WELCOME TO Pump Street Primary

Meet some of the children ...

Barry Barsby

Daisy Poborski

Rashid Ali

Floella Potts

Freddie Stanton

Monica Bellis

... in Miss Twigg's class

Craig Soapy

Karen Smart

Terry Flynn

Fatima Patel

Lily Wongsam

Paul Dimbley

THIS IS BOB WILSON

He wrote this story
and drew the pictures.

He lives in the Derbyshire countryside in a
house which he designed and built himself
from an old cowshed. He has three grown-up
children and nine grandchildren. When he
was young he wanted to be a pop star, and
he started to write songs. He became an art
teacher and wrote plays and musicals, and
shows for television and radio. Then he began
to write and illustrate stories for children. He
is the author of the *Stanley Bagshaw* picture
books and the best-selling *Ging Gang Goolie,
It's an Alien!*

First published 2000 by Macmillan Children's Books
a division of Macmillan Publishers Limited
25 Eccleston Place, London SW1W 9NF
Basingstoke and Oxford
www.macmillan.co.uk

Associated companies throughout the world

ISBN 0 330 37094 4

1 3 5 7 9 8 6 4 2

A CIP catalogue record for this book is available from
the British Library.

Printed and bound in Great Britain by Mackays of Chatham plc, Kent

Visit Bob Wilson's website at www.planetbob.co.uk

written and illustrated by
Bob Wilson

MACMILLAN CHILDREN'S BOOKS

Here are some of the school staff ...

Mr C Warrilow BSc MEd

Miss Twigg

Mr Manley

Mr Boggis

Mrs York

Mr Lamp-Williams

Miss Gaters

Mrs Jellie

Norman Loops

Janice

Mrs Brazil

For Ami, Thomas, Elias,
Matilda, Reuben, Alexander,
Marius, Lucien and Babik

THIS IS FLOELLA POTTS

We call her Flo.
Flo is the smallest girl in our class.

Sometimes people call Flo other things.
They call her "Titch" or "Shorty" or
"the mighty midget". She
doesn't seem to mind.
Miss Twigg, our teacher,
says that Flo has got a
very positive attitude.

I'm not really very small,
Miss. Everyone else just
happens to be bigger.

Being very small can be a problem. For example, it's not always easy to do someone a little favour.

And it's often hard to get yourself noticed.

But Flo has got what Miss Twigg calls
"an indomitable spirit".
(I think she means she never gives up.)

And she makes sure she doesn't get
overlooked.

But the worst thing about being small is that people think it's perfectly all right to make jokes about your size. And sometimes it isn't.

For example, one day in class Miss Twigg was telling us about the different sorts of jobs we might choose to do when we left school.

Jane Walley said, "Please, Miss, when I leave school I'm going to be a ballet dancer."

People say I've got loads and loads of natural charm.

"That's nice," said Miss Twigg.
(*Jane Walley is quite fat and rather clumsy – but nobody ever mentions that in case she gets upset.*)

Then Nicola Boot said, "Please, Miss. I'm going to be a supermodel."

People say I've got an obvious talent.

"That's interesting," said Miss Twigg. (*Nicola Boot is quite big and very gawky – but nobody ever says anything in case she gets offended.*) And then Miss Twigg said, "What about you, Flo?"

Have you got a special ambition?

"Yes, Miss. I have," said Flo.

I would like to be a professional netball player.

"You'll never be a professional netball player," said Nicola.
"Certainly not," said Jane.
"Why not?" said Flo.
"You've not got what it takes," said Nicola.
"You've got no natural talent," said Jane.
"In other words," said Nicola and Jane.

You're too small!

Miss Twigg said, "I tell you what, Flo. I could have a word with your mother."

Tell her to put some cow manure in your shoes. You never know — it might help you to grow a bit faster.

and everyone laughed.

Except for Flo.

Flo didn't think it was funny.
When Miss Twigg saw that Flo wasn't
laughing Miss Twigg didn't think it was
very funny either. She said, "All right.
That's enough." And sent everyone back
to their places.
When everyone had settled down, she
said,

**Flo. I'm sorry. I
didn't think.**

Then she turned to the rest of us and said,

There is absolutely no reason why Flo can't be a professional netball player.

She said that to succeed in life a person needed to have more than just talent and charm . . . and height. They needed to have what Flo had got, and that was a positive attitude. She said that a person with a positive attitude could go a long way.
And she was very nearly right because a few weeks later, Flo very nearly went

A really **REALLY** *LONG WAY!*

Miss Twigg said, "Gather round, everybody. I've got something to show you."

Inside this cylinder is a special gas called helium.

She said we must pay attention. We were going to learn why helium gas was special.

I am now filling this balloon with helium gas.

Now I'm tying it with string.

Then Miss Twigg held the balloon up in the air and said, "Now watch this."
And then she let it go.
It didn't fall.

It floated.

Up into the sky.

Helium gas was special because it was lighter than air.

When we were back in the classroom
we found out why Miss Twigg wanted
us to know about helium being lighter
than air.

This year Miss Twigg was going to
organise

She had already worked out the rules.

GRAND BALLOON RACE

SPRING FÊTE   Saturday 3rd May

RULES

To enter the race children must purchase a pre-printed luggage label.

GRAND BALLOON RACE

Name of sender · · · · · · · · · · · · · · · · · · ·

Name of finder · · · · · · · · · · · · · · · · · · ·

Where found ·

Please return this label by 6th June to
Pump Street Primary School

Cost: 50p (Only one label allowed per child) Children then write their name – in capital letters – on the label.

On the day of the fête each completed label will be attached to a helium-filled balloon.

At 4pm ALL the balloons will be released.

The balloon which has travelled the greatest distance as indicated by 'Where found' on the returned label will win a prize.

Competition closes on Monday 6th June (Balloon labels returned after that date won't count.)

"What do you think?" said Miss Twigg.
We said we thought it was a good idea.
But a few days later Miss Twigg had

AN EVEN BETTER IDEA

She said that instead of writing our names on a label and tying it to the balloon, why didn't we write a proper letter asking whoever found our balloon to write a letter back. That way we might get ourselves a pen pal.
Miss Twigg said,

D'you think you could do that?

And everyone replied,

Yes, Miss. Easy, Miss. No problem.

She handed out some note paper and we started to write our letters.

But it's hard to write a letter when you
don't know who you're writing to.
And after a few minutes Rashid Ali
said, "Please, Miss, can you help me?
I'm a bit stuck."
Miss Twigg said,

Is anyone else a
bit stuck?

And everyone replied,

Yes, Miss. Me, Miss. It's dead hard.

So Miss Twigg told us all to gather
round and she gave us some help.

Miss Twigg had already drawn up a plan. First of all we had to say who we were.

Next space on the list was for our hobbies. Miss Twigg asked us for examples of what we might put here. Julie Abberton said, "Disco dancing." Craig Soapy said, "Watching TV." "Very good," said Miss Twigg, and as each of us suggested a hobby she wrote it down on a flip chart.

We did the same thing for what we looked like, and what our ambitions were. Each time one of us thought of an example Miss Twigg wrote it down on the chart.

MY NAME
I HAVE
MY HOBBIES
DANCIN TV
I WAN BE A
NC ALLER

How about a vet, Miss?

She said we didn't have to follow her plan exactly. It was just meant as a guide. She said, "Have you got the idea?"
And everybody* replied,

Yes, Miss. Got it, Miss. No worries.

*Well *nearly* everybody.

Karen Smart was the first to finish.

I expect my balloon will travel millions of miles, Miss.

MY NAME IS KAREN SMART. I've got JET BLACK HAIR. My hobby is knowing a lot of big words. I am what's called ~~Nolligab~~ ~~intellict~~ very clever. If this balloon lands in a far off distant country and you can't read it cuz you're forrin you can still write back because I know lots of forrin words too
BONJOUR SPAGGETEE
Karen Smart
PS This is Spanish. It means 'goodbye'.

"What d'you think?" said Karen.
"It's . . . er . . . interesting," said Miss Twigg.

Flo was next to hand in her letter.
She said, "Is it all right, Miss?"

Hello!

My name is Floella Potts but most people call me Flo. I am 7 yrs old. I like going swimming and doing sport. My favourite sport is netball. My ambition is to play netball for England. But I don't often tell people about this because they make fun of me because of my height – and this makes me feel a bit lonely.

I would really like to have a pen pal. So please write back.

Flo Potts X

It's a very nice letter,

said Miss Twigg.

Soon everybody* had finished their letter and handed it in to Miss Twigg.

*Well, *nearly* everybody.

When the bell went for the end of school Rashid had still hardly started. "Look, Rashid, it's easy," said Miss Twigg.

All you've got to do is follow my plan.

She told Rashid that he could finish his letter at home. She said that if he just wrote down what it said on her plan he couldn't go far wrong.

Because Rashid Ali is a good boy who always does as he is told.
Miss Twigg said he should just write what it said on her plan.

So that's *exactly* what he did.

MY NAME IS . . . .
Put your name here

I HAVE red/curly
blonde/black hair

MY HOBBIES ARE disco
dancing, TV, autograph
unting, sKateboard

I WANT TO BE A

pop star

Everybody was looking forward to the Spring Fête – and not just because of the balloon race. There would be lots of other things to see and do.

Last year the main attraction had been a puppet show.
This year there was going to be something even better. It was

"Bouncy castles are brilliant," said Nicola.
"Absolutely fantastic," said Jane.

I've never had a go on a bouncy castle,

said Flo.

ON THE DAY OF THE FÊTE

all the teachers were very busy. Miss Twigg was setting up the stand for a grand balloon race. She had got herself into a bit of a tizz.

To be honest, I'm not sure how I'm going to cope.

"Could I be of any help?" said Flo. Miss Twigg said that Flo could be a really *big* help. She gave her the microphone to hold, and said,

You can be my Chief Announcer.

Then Barry Barsby offered to help too.

I could hold the balloons.

So did Julie Abberton.

I could tie the labels.

Nicola and Jane wanted to know what was going on.
"We're helping Miss Twigg," said Barry.
"We're the Balloon Race team," said Jane.
        "You can help too, if you like,"
        said Flo.

But Nicola and Jane didn't want to help Miss Twigg. They wanted to go on the bouncy castle.

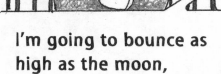

I'm going to bounce as high as the sun,

said Nicola.

I'm going to bounce as high as the moon,

said Jane.

Me too,

said Flo.

I've always wanted to have a go on a bouncy castle.

"Mr Bobble won't let you go on his bouncy castle," said Nicola.
"Certainly not," said Jane.
"Why not?" said Flo.
"Because . . ." said Nicola and Jane.

You're too . . .

Too what?

said Miss Twigg.

said Nicola.

And then they both ran off giggling.

"Take no notice, Flo," said Miss Twigg.

Flo decided she was going to enjoy being the Chief Balloon Race Announcer. She said,

Hey listen, Barry. This megaphone makes me sound as if I'm . . .

REALLY BIG!

She could be heard all over the school. Even in the infants' playground.

ROLL UP . . . ROLL UP!

IN THE INFANTS' PLAYGROUND

Nicola and Jane were waiting to have a go on the bouncy castle.

I'm going to have a hundred goes, said Nicola.

I'm going to have a thousand goes, said Jane.

"Sorry, girls," said Mr Bobble.

You're not going to have any goes.

said Nicola.

said Jane.

"Because," said Mr Bobble, "the bouncy castle is for little ones only. And you're both"

OUT ON THE FOOTBALL FIELD

The Balloon Race team were working well. People were queuing up to enter the race.

Miss Twigg took the money and checked that the label had been filled in properly. Jane tied the label to a balloon and handed it over to Barry. Soon Barry was holding quite a big bunch of balloons.

IT WAS THREE O'CLOCK

and every one of the balloons had now
got a label or a letter tied to it.
At ten to four Flo was to announce that
the balloon race would start in ten
minutes. There was not much to do
until then.
"I'm just going to have a word with Mr
Boggis," said Miss Twigg.
She said she'd only be five minutes. She
said she hoped that Barry could be
trusted not to do anything silly while
she was away. And just to make certain
that he could be trusted she said,
"Barry, if you let go of those balloons
before 4 o'clock . . ."

I'll **have your guts
for garters**.

IT WAS NEARLY TEN TO FOUR

and Barry Barsby was getting a bit fed up. Just standing about holding a bunch of balloons was really boring. He fancied having a go on the megaphone.

So he said, "Hey, Flo. D'you know, holding these helium balloons is really good fun."

They're so floaty. Look how they're pulling my arm up. It's like I'm flying.

Could I have a try?

said Flo.

Barry said, "Er . . . well . . . oh, all right." Flo could have a go with the balloons if he could have a go with the megaphone. They could do a swap. But remembering Miss Twigg's threat, he said, "Whatever happens . . ."

DON'T LET GO!

"Don't worry," said Flo. "I won't."

IT WAS TEN TO FOUR

and Miss Twigg was by the bike sheds chatting to Mr Boggis when she heard the announcement.

Yes. It's gone very well.

She was expecting to hear Flo Potts say, "Ladies and Gentlemen. The Grand Balloon Race will start in ten minutes." But what she did hear was Barry Barsby say

LADIES AND GENTLEMAN. OH NO! CRIKEY! COME BACK!

It could only mean one thing.

"No, Miss," said Barry.

"Flo's got them, Miss," said Barry.

Barry didn't reply. He wasn't sure what he should say.

Miss Twigg said, "You lot. Come here. I need your help."

Flo has gone missing. I need to find her quickly. She's got the balloons.

Nobody moved.
"Well, come on. Chop chop," said Miss Twigg.

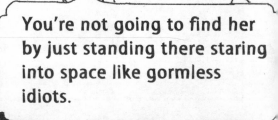

You're not going to find her by just standing there staring into space like gormless idiots.

Still nobody moved.

What's the matter? What are you all staring at?

When at last Miss Twigg saw what we were staring at, and realised what the matter was, she didn't move either. She just said, "Oh, my sainted aunt!" And then stood staring into space like a gormless idiot.

Please, Miss,

said Flo.

Miss Twigg didn't reply. She wasn't sure
what she should say.

When she'd been training to be a teacher she'd been given a very useful book. It was called

THE TRAINEE TEACHER'S PHRASE BOOK

The things a good teacher should, and should not, say.

Part 3: Your questions answered

Q A seven-year-old boy in my class tends to get overexcited and do stupid things. I've tried saying, "Now calm down, William," but this has no effect. What *should* I say?

A You should say, "How old are you?" If the boy replies, "I'm seven, Miss," you should then say, "Well, then, *act your age!*" (However much tempted, you should *not* say, "Do you want to be eight?")

Q An eight-year-old girl in my class keeps shutting the window just after I've opened it. I've tried saying, "Joanne, if you're feeling cold you should tell me." But she still does it. What should I say?

A You should say, "Did I tell you to do that?" When the girl replies, "No, Miss," you should then say, "Well, I'm telling you now – don't do it!" (However much tempted, you should *not* say, "or you'll get a thick ear!")

the girl replies, "No, Miss," you should
then say, "Well, I'm telling you now – don't do
it!"

(However much tempted, you should *not* say, "or
you'll get a thick ear!")

Q Supposing I discover that one of my pupils is
hanging from a bunch of helium-filled balloons
30 metres up in the air, it looks like the wind is
getting up, and she asks if it's time for her to let
go of the balloons yet. What should I say?

A The situation you have described is what we edu-
cationalists call A Dire Emergency.

In A Dire Emergency you should use the phrase
to be found on page 272 in the chapter called,
"What to Say in A Dire Emergency."

Barry Barsby said,

It's 4 o'clock, Miss. Shall
I tell Flo to release the
balloons?

Miss Twigg didn't reply. She was trying
to remember exactly what it said on
page 272.

Karen Smart said,

Barry, you shouldn't bother Miss Twigg with questions. Can't you see she's thinking. She's got a lot to think about. This is clearly a dire emergency.

If Flo lets go of the balloons now, she'll almost certainly break every bone in her body.

"On the other hand," said Karen, "if she doesn't let go, and the wind gets up . . ."

She'd remembered the phrase that was on page 272 of her really useful book. She knew what she was supposed to say in a dire emergency. And she said it. She said,

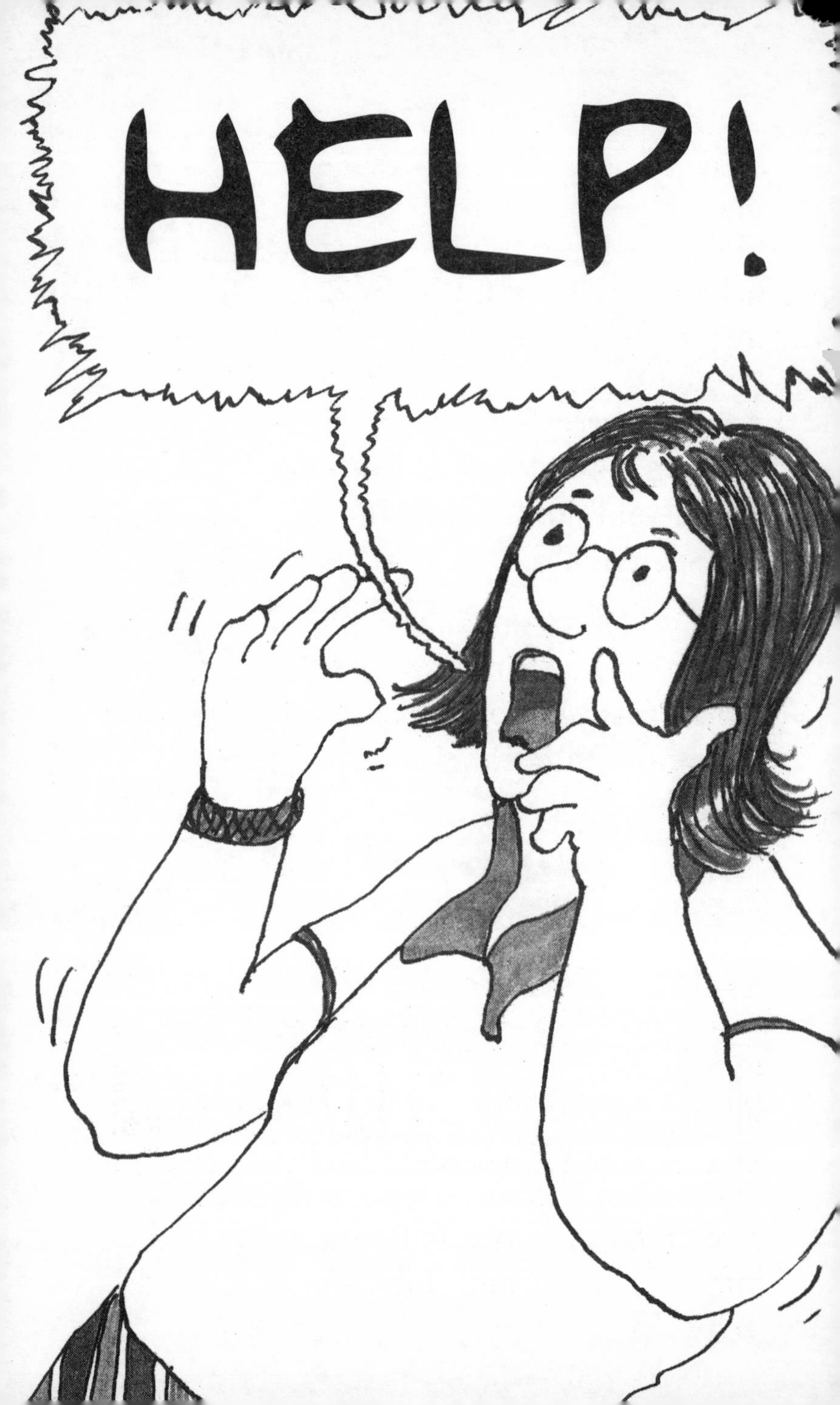
HELP!

At this point Craig Soapy said something really useful. He said, "I once saw this TV programme about how they make films. There was this helicopter flying really high and these men started to fight and one of them fell out of the door and he screamed Aaaaiiiiieeeee!"

But he didn't hurt himself because he was really a stuntman and they'd put this great big bouncy cushion thing underneath for him to land on.

Noticing that Flo was floating over the infants' playground, Lily Wongsam said,

"So do I," said Barry.

But Miss Twigg said, "No! She mustn't let go! If she lets go now . . ."

She'll break every bone in her body!

But she did let go.

And she didn't break every bone
in her body because she landed on

Mr Bobble's Bouncy Castle.

And she

BOUNCED

and she

BOUNCED

AND SHE

BOUNCED

It's not fair!

said Nicola.

Not fair at all!

said Jane.

By the time Flo had stopped bouncing the balloons carrying our letters had sailed up into the sky and were disappearing into the distance.

the first letter arrived. It was addressed to Karen Smart.

I expect it's come from some far-off foreign land,

said Karen.

"I think perhaps you should read it," said Miss Twigg.
Karen read her letter.

And then, because Miss Twigg asked her to, she read it out to the rest of the class.

Dear Karen,

It was nice to get a letter from you. Mind you, it was only by chance that I got it. Mrs Benge (from no. 14) found it at the bottom of her garden tied to a balloon! She gave it to me when she saw me at the Post Office.

You can write again if you like, but next time why not just pop your letter through the letter box. After all, I only live next door.

    X love your gran X

PS I didn't know you spoke forin.

the second letter arrived. It had been posted in Manchester. Miss Twigg read the name on the envelope.

Then she said,

> Rashid. I think this is probably meant for you.

Rashid read his letter.

It said

Dear Putyour,

I am 7 years old. My dad gave me your letter. He's a steward at Old Trafford. Your balloon came down in the middle of the pitch just as we were about to kick off against Arsenal. My hobbies are supporting Man Utd (of course) and doing things on my PC - like this letter. Your hobby sounds really interesting.

What does a red/blonde/black-haired footballing autograph-hunting TV disco vet do exactly?

Your new pal,

askar Madvod

S I've asked my dad if he can
t you some of the Man Utd
yers' autographs.)

Crikey!

Soon lots of letters started arriving.
They came from all sorts of interesting
places.

Miss Twigg worked out that so far Lily
Wongsam was in the lead. Her balloon
had travelled nearly 200 miles. But it
was too soon to declare her the winner.
The competition didn't close until the
6th of June and there was still one more
letter to come.

we had a special assembly. Mr Warrilow, the head teacher, had an announcement to make. It was the 6th of June – and the last letter had arrived. Someone's balloon had travelled all the way across the Irish Sea to a little village called Ballydonegal.

A distance of over three hundred and fifty miles!

It was the winning letter. And the name on the envelope was . . .

Flo was called up on stage to collect her prize. And also her letter.

Flo read her letter. It *was* interesting.

It said

llo Flo,

y name is Joe, I'm 9 yrs old. Your balloon
ame down in my garden. I'm glad it did
ecause I would like to be your pen friend. I
hink we could be really good friends because we
ure so much alike.
For a start, I like sports too, like you. At school
we play a game called hurling which is a bit like
hockey. But it's not my favourite sport. My
favourite sport is horse riding. When I grow up
I'd like to be a National Hunt Jockey.
I understand when you say about people always
making fun of you because of your height. It's
exactly the same for me. See how much alike we
are!

Write back soon. Your new friend,
                    Joe Locke

PS I've sent a photo of me. I'm the one with
the curly hair, second from the right.

But the most interesting thing about the
letter was

the photo!

THE END

DANGEROUS DAISY

Miss Twigg wants the head teacher to get a surprise on his birthday. Thanks to Daisy . . .

He gets a REALLY BIG surprise!

Daisy's not a naughty girl. But she does tend to blow things up.

BARRY'S BEAR

When Miss Twigg takes her class on a trip to a nature park she doesn't expect the wildlife to be quite so wild.

It was HUGE and HAIRY and very, very SCARY!

And it ate my strawberry yoghurt.

Football Fred

Fred's a dancer, not a goalie. When Miss Twigg picks him for the match against St Mildred's, he says

I'll do the best I can, Miss.

But will Fred's best be good enough?

YES!

MONICA'S MONSTER

Miss Twigg likes animals. But when Monica brings little Samantha to school and says

Please, Miss, would you like to see my pet?

Miss Twigg says

NO!

PUMP STREET PRIMARY
titles available from Macmillan

1. Dangerous Daisy	0 330 37092 8	£3.50
2. Barry's Bear	0 330 37090 1	£3.50
3. Flying Flo	0 330 37094 4	£3.50
4. Football Fred	0 330 37091 X	£3.50
5. Monica's Monster	0 330 37093 6	£3.50
6. Rashid's Rescue	0 330 37095 2	£3.50
